The Un-circle of Life

Terry James

Published by Growingknowing, 2023.

The Un-circle of Life

Table of Contents

I dedicate this play to my father, Dr. Sydney James, who spent his life teaching literature and theatre.

List characters

Celeste - siren
Sartre – waiter
Leonardo (Leo) - artist
Fyodor - rebel
Hypatia -intellectual
Bill - capitalist

ACT I

Expensive hotel — early evening.

An elegantly dressed woman, about 18, walks with two canes and some difficulty to the table in the room's center. She sits facing the entrance, hides her canes under the table, and strikes a few poses to ensure the most seductive impression on anyone entering the room. she undoes a top button on her dress and crosses her legs to reveal a long slit in the dress. She is alone in the room. the furniture and decorations are sumptuous, with lots of red velvet cushions and wallpaper, candles, and chandeliers.

Sundry noises emerge off-stage as someone moves about with some urgency and muffled talk. A waiter enters the room from behind a Chinese silk screen at the rear. He is pushing a laden cart and is looking down at a squeaky wheel.

WAITER: Oh. I did not see you. We do not open for 20 minutes. Did you not notice the door was roped off?

CELESTE: (*smiling*) I entered early to get the best seat. I hope you can forgive me? (*The waiter stares at her for much too long*).

WAITER: Sorry, Madam. I lost myself for a moment.

CELESTE: I never tire of attention. I should be sick of it by now, but I love every second glance more than the first.

WAITER: (*flustered*) Can I get you anything, Madam?

CELESTE: MADAM! Please do not call me Madam. I am Celeste. Madam is for dowagers and curmudgeons.

WAITER: Can I get you anything, Celeste?

CELESTE: Anything? Hmm. I need to think about it. Anything comes in so many shapes and colors.

WAITER: We have mulled hot cider. It comes with a cinnamon stick, and it is free. (*He fumbles in his pocket and pulls out a bowtie*). Oh, no. I am not wearing my tie. (*He struggles to make a bowtie knot using a kettle as a mirror*).

CELESTE: Cider sounds more like a *something* than an *anything?* Is it really free?

WAITER: Oh, yes. No charge, Mada... Celeste.

CELESTE: No charge at all? Doesn't the High Tea cost $140? Is it possible the free cider is included in the high cost of the high tea? McDonalds has a one-dollar tea. Perhaps the *free* cider is not *really* free?

WAITER: Your one-dollar tea does not include a beautiful flower that opens slowly as you drink. Our tea is magnificent. Our tea comes with real cream, scones, salmon and cucumber sandwiches, apricots, desserts, and sunny smiles.

CELESTE: Can I have just the free cider and skip the tea?

WAITER: Oh, no. The cider is only for guests who buy the High Tea.

CELESTE: Hmm. (*Celeste gives him a knowing nod*).

WAITER: I have the cider right here.

CELESTE: I would love a warm cider. Please forgive my behavior. (*She plays with her pearl necklace. The waiter stares at her cleavage for longer than he should. He dabbles around the cart and puts a cup of cider before her*). Do you like my pearls?

WAITER: Your dress is intriguing. The fabric is so intricate, and the lace so ornate. It looks like the best lace I have seen.

CELESTE: Just my dress? (*She giggles. She puts her hand under the dress and pulls it out*). The dress is diaphanous. You are looking at the lace camisole beneath this transparent floral fabric. Is it the dress that is so intriguing, or perhaps something warm and cuddly inside the dress? (*The waiter turns red, shuffles his feet like a schoolboy, and escapes behind the screen. She giggles again*).

The front door swings open. Leo walks in wearing a tuxedo. He has DARK hair, a moustache, and an athletic build. He is around 27. Leo limps with a stiff right leg to celeste.

CELESTE: My darling Leonardo. You are so dapper in your tux.

LEO: I am playing at a club later. (*He takes her hand and kisses it*). You are still the beauty amongst beauties. Will you break my heart again tonight?

CELESTE: Don't sit so far away. Come sit next to me.

LEO: The last time I sat next to you... things got out of control. You kept patting my leg more with every glass of champagne.

CELESTE: It was a most delicious evening. As I recall, you followed me into a stairwell. You grabbed my wrists and held them above my head with one hand. You kissed me so passionately I could barely stand. I forgot where I was, who I was, and what I was doing. It was a kiss to remember for ten lifetimes. It makes me shiver thinking about it.

LEO: Exactly. This is why I am sitting over here. (*Celeste takes a sugar cube and throws it at his mouth. Leo catches it with a flip of his head*).

CELESTE: Have you learned more instruments? What do you play now?

LEO: Classical guitar, Spanish guitar, and jazz guitar. Double bass. Violin. I added mandolin, piano, and of course, the fool.

CELESTE: I am not familiar with that last one. Do you play any wind instruments?

LEO: Harmonica. Is the Kazoo an instrument?

CELESTE: I don't remember the violin.

LEO: I don't really play the violin. I play around on the violin. If you cannot make a living with an instrument, you are not a professional. You are just playing around. Enough about me, did you marry anyone new? How many times have you been married now?

CELESTE: Ten or so. I stopped counting at ten. Too embarrassing.

LEO: Ten!

CELESTE: The last time I married, the forms asked for a name and date for every prior marriage. Oh God, how can they expect me to remember everyone I've married? The look that woman gave me when I told her there was not enough space on the form to list them all. Eventually, I told her it was impossible. When I approached the counter, she called me, "My dear." When I left, she gave me a scowl that would turn Medusa to stone.

LEO: People don't understand us.

CELESTE: I am free and single now. Imagine the fun we'd have if you sat closer.

FYODOR enters the front door. Fyodor turns back, cracks open the door an inch, looking outside. He opens the door wider, sticks his head out, AND scans the road back and forth.

He has curly hair, a red beard, and blue eyes. He is 200 pounds, about 50, six feet, and large. He is dressed in black pants, A black shirt, and blue cowboy boots. He uses crutches with amazing speed as he zooms over to the table, zigzagging AND SPINNING between the chairs.

LEO: Fyodor, it has been too long. What an unexpected pleasure to see you. Last I heard, you were in prison in Iran.

FYODOR: Not the best prison, but better than many.

WAITER: Hot cider, anyone? It is free.

LEO: I would love a hot cider.

FYODOR: I also need a cider, aaaaaand... I need a large snifter of your cheapest brandy.

CELESTE: Let me buy you the smoothest brandy, Fyodor. A celebration for your unexpected release.

FYODOR: Much as I love you, Celeste, I must decline. On a cold day, I prefer cheap brandy. The liquid must not melt like chocolate. No, I want the brandy to sting and tingle on my frozen lips so I can feel them again. I like that slow glowing burn as the brandy drips down to my stomach. A cheap brandy is perfect on a cold December day.

WAITER: Of course, Sir. Right away. Our very cheapest brandy.

FYODOR: That young fool was talking to me but looking at you, Celeste. I think you have captured another heart to add to your innumerable trophies. Cardiologists should pay you for all those broken hearts. (*Celeste leans over, squeezes Fyodor's cheek, then smooths his beard*).

CELESTE: You are still a romantic despite all those years in prison. How many jails, how many years of incarceration?

FYODOR: Hundreds. Iran was for protesting the development of nuclear weapons. Imagine, a theocracy developing weapons of mass destruction. The irony of a spiritual leader killing millions was too unbearable. Does the Supreme Religious Leader scratch his arse when he prays to God? Someone, perhaps a Russian writer, told me that.

LEO: I think it was Dostoevsky.

FYODOR: No, I don't know him. It was something I read. After all the beatings, I cannot remember... Before that, I was imprisoned in Russia for demanding fair elections. Earlier, I was in jail for protesting the death penalty in Texas. They kill so many prisoners in Texas they need an electric bench, not an electric chair. State-sanctioned murder.

CELESTE: Not murder. You mean punishment for terrible their crimes, surely?

FYODOR: When they discovered DNA as evidence, half the prisoners on death row at the time were found to be innocent. For the innocent 50%, it was state-sanctioned murder. Ah, my brandy arrives. (*He lifts the glass up high, then sips slowly*). The years blend together. A new country, a new outrage, and a new jail.

LEO: Why fight against injustice across the entire world? Fyodor, are there not enough crimes against humanity in our own nation? You cannot boil the ocean.

FYODOR: I try not to get arrested at home, so I can come home when things get wicked. Fortunately, I always escape, eventually.

CELESTE: We are so glad to have our justice warrior return. You are the consummate rebel.

The door opens. Hypatia swirls in. She is a tall, elegant woman, about 40. She is wearing a flowing white chiffon dress with a royal blue diagonal stripe, A blue knee-length cape, a gold necklace, and high heels. Holding the door for her, Bill follows. He is a short, chubby man in his early forties wearing an expensive Italian white wool suit and white patent leather shoes. Bill has a leg brace and walks with a clicking sound. Hypatia swirls the cape across her legs and moves smoothly to the table.

HYPATIA: My test subjects. You are so dear to me. I want to embrace each one of you. You are living proof my theories work. (*Hypatia presses her cheek against both cheeks of each person at the table*).

BILL: An afternoon tea with drinks for everyone – my treat.

CELESTE: I love bubbles. Bubbles are more fun.

LEO: Is a high tea the same as an afternoon tea?

FYODOR: Who cares? Tea is tea.

CELESTE: Don't tell the waiter. He will give you a soliloquy about opening flowers as you drink an exquisite magnificent beverage of the heavens. I have been dying to ask if we all know our spirit animal? I think mine would be a panda.

LEO: A lion?

FYODOR: Everyone has a lovely spirit. I might be a hyena, although dictators might suggest Ebola as a good fit for me.

BILL: I suppose a shark? Not a nasty shark, a reasonable shark you can negotiate with... a shark with a colossal appetite yet a kind heart.

HYPATIA: A reasonable shark is an oxymoron, Bill. I would pick human as my spirit animal with a 99% confidence level and a 1% margin of error. I like humans, mainly in the abstract... My best friends are definitely humans.

FYODOR: Really. Your best friends are human. Who would have guessed?

CELESTE: If most of your friends are human, what are the other friends. Aliens? Dogs? Please say, dogs.

HYPATIA: Robots, of course. I love data, artificial intelligence, and robots. Those naughty little nanobots are so adorable. They always surprise you with their quirks.

CELESTE: I thought the spirit animal idea would allow me to see the hidden dimension of my closest friends. That was a bust and a bit scary. Sometimes, it is better to keep the hidden side hidden. Put that whole revelation into a deeply, deeper depth of the unfathomably deep unconscious subconscious.

LEO: Do your robots have a name and everything?

HYPATIA: All my friends have a name and everything. I said my best friends are human. Although, that might change? Robots are so intelligent, excellent listeners, and really fun. If you have a terrible robot, just write some code and fix him.

CELESTE: I like men, even if I can't always fix them, and they don't always listen.

HYPATIA: Well, I listen. In fact, I want to hear from each of you. It has been 10 years since our last meeting. What have you done?

LEO: Why don't you start, Hypatia?

HYPATIA: My focus is following your namesake, Leonardo Da Vinci. The Renaissance ideal. I was born in the wrong era. Genetic engineering was my first love. I have added artificial intelligence, machine learning, and nanobots. So many opportunities are missed if you cannot see the layers and systemic interplay between subjects. I have completed a Ph.D. in mathematics, genetics, synthetic biology, computer science, regenerative medicine, and medicine. I want to learn it all. My love of learning grows in spirals and loops as boundaries evaporate when I slowly peel back Nature's secrets like the layers of an onion. Nature closely guards her secrets, but I love finding her mysteries and learning her complexities.

CELESTE: You are in love but did not mention a man? A decade of learning and not one deep stare into the eyes of a man suffering to be closer to you?

HYPATIA: Einstein described the happiest thought of his life when he realized the impact of gravity within an accelerating frame of reference instead of an inert frame.

CELESTE: What? His happiest moment was not when he met his wife or married his true love? The birth of his child was not his happiest moment? The happiest moment is a moving frame of reference! I am missing out.

HYPATIA: Exactly. You understand.

FYODOR: Well, I don't.

HYPATIA: Celeste, your last spouse. Did he love you?

CELESTE: Yes. He loved me at the beginning.

HYPATIA: Using what frame of reference? Did he love you more than his mother? Did he love you more than his dog, car, or god?

CELESTE: Yes, to mother, yes to the dog, but no, to his car. He did not love me more than his car. As soon as he gave that little red convertible the name *Baby*, I should have realized things had changed. When he spent more time cleaning, driving, and doting over his car, I still did not see I was replaced. I am wiser. He loves me, but how do I compare to a shiny chrome bumper? Boys and their toys.

LEO: Love can be cruel. My saddest moment today was listening to Celeste explain the automobile frame of reference.

HYPATIA: It is more common than most people think. According to one study, if men have to choose between keeping their car or their wife, 60% of men prefer their car.

FYODOR: Hell, yes. I expect the car complains less and may smell better. The car also gives you the benefit of transportation.

CELESTE: I have taken many men where they want to go.

BILL: You had a vow he would love you until death, Celeste. You have his signature on a marriage contract. You can sue him and be rich.

CELESTE: The contract said he'd love me until *death do us part*, and when I ran down the driveway waving the contract, he laughed and kept driving. The contract did not help me. I was still alone and crying on the front lawn. I loved him so much; I chased after him before I had a chance to put on my lipstick.

LEO: Oh no; how dreadful!

CELESTE: I know, right!

BILL: ...but you are rich?

CELESTE: Yes. I live like a goddess.

BILL: You should let me make your investments, Celeste.

FYODOR: How long were you married?

CELESTE: I don't remember. We had a 60th anniversary, then things changed. He got bored. He was less passionate and had lower energy in his eighties.

FYODOR: Sixty years of married bliss sounds good. Sixty years of love is excellent. Few men over 80 have three specks of passion or two grams of energy.

CELESTE: Leo has energy. We all do.

LEO: Hypatia. Peel back that onion. Give me an example of your insights.

HYPATIA: If you could be ten times as strong, intelligent, kind, happy, handsome, and healthy. If you could be physically, emotionally, and mentally your best times ten. You could achieve the ancient Greek ideal -a strong mind in a strong body. You'd be your very best. The best of the best, the "crème de la crème", to quote Jean Brodie. This is my goal.

FYODOR: A superhuman?

HYPATIA: Well, yes. A genetic transhuman, the elevation of progress, an accelerated evolution.

BILL: But Hypatia, did you spend no time solving the glucose browning problem in our joints. We have young bodies and pulsing hormones. We have the high energy and spirits of a teenager but old joints. We cannot walk five steps without a struggle. I would kill to have working joints. My strong heart will let me run up a mountain. My joints and tendons won't let me walk ten yards to the kitchen without canes or braces on my knees.

LEO: Why are you calling it a transhuman? I thought scientists always used Greek symbols and Latin words to sound more intelligent. If you use Greek symbols, that instantly makes you more intelligent and more educated, doesn't it?

HYPATIA: I did.

LEO: Transhuman sounds like English.

HYPATIA: The Latin for Transhuman is *transhumana*.

LEO: Oh. You're right; it sounds the same. I was expecting *magnum opus homosapien trascendento*. You know how scientists like to call some beetle the magnum-negro-Hercules as a fancy way of saying the giant, black, strong beetle. I wish they would use English names.

FYODOR: Hey, Leo. You and I can think of a name with a bit more punch than a transhuman.

CELESTE: Sorry, I was daydreaming. What is a transhuman, someone in transit, like taking a bus?

FYODOR: I think a trans-person is a person who switches gender. A guy who dresses up like a woman has transitioned.

CELESTE: He might dress like a woman, but doesn't that make him a man in a dress?

LEO: Old thinking, my dear Celeste. Gender is not an on-off switch. We have shades of gray between black and white. He might be a woman trapped in a man's body.

HYPATIA: Trans-human is where we have enhanced human DNA with genes that are not part of the human gene pool. For example, we alter the human DNA to make someone have a better immune system by taking DNA from a pig, dog, or bat. We can make humans kinder by taking DNA from a pigeon.

BILL: Pigeons are kind? They poop on my car all the time. I think they do it on purpose. I think they aim.

HYPATIA: Have you ever seen an attack pigeon? Do you see pigeons tearing the flesh of some small animal? No. They are gentle to other animals.

FYODOR: Animals. You cannot mix human DNA with animals. That is obscene.

CELESTE: I don't see why, Fyodor. I met some of your friends who seemed closer to animals, given how they gawked at me.

FYODOR: True. Some of my best friends act like animals when they are drunk. However, I don't want some woman with vampire bat ears chirping and tweeting to get radar signals while she sucks blood from my toe.

HYPATIA: Bats have the best immune system in the animal kingdom. Bats shrug off nearly any disease – polio, measles, herpes, or smallpox. You would be lucky to have a bat immune system enhancement.

CELESTE: Hypatia, I love your idea of the Greek ideal man. I would love to have an ideal man right now. Someone with big, tight firm buttocks.

BILL: Look, Celeste. I have firm buttocks. I keep my fat wallet in my back pocket, and look how big and firm my butt is. (*He pulls up his blazer and slaps his buttock*).

LEO: I understand that Greeks have many words for love. *Agape* is the love of God. *Philia* is the love of a friend.

CELESTE: I like *eros*, the romantic, passionate love.

LEO: ...and *storge*, the love of your family such as your mother or brother.

HYPATIA: Don't forget *nous*, intellect as the love of knowledge.

WAITER: Forgive my interruption, but a Greek friend told me *nous* is an ancient Greek word. No one says *nous* anymore.

FYODOR: Could that explain why Greece is no longer the intellectual leader of the world?

WAITER: If a society has many words for a thing like love, that says something about a culture. The more important the concept is for the community, the more terms we want to allow us to distinguish nuances. We have so many negative words: hate, detest, disgust, abhor, loathe, despise, averse, and repulse... do you think that means we are not as nice as the ancient Greeks? (*He swirls a four-tiered silver platter with many gourmet offerings to each person. With a flourish, he puts out various teapots, each with unique flavors. He places bottles of champagne in ice buckets about the table. The waiter is particularly attentive to Celeste, exchanging smiles often. They all are silent as they watch the waiter's performance).*

HYPATIA: Look at this lovely display of food. Please tell me more. Please tell me tell me about your triumphs, your failures, and your goals.

FYODOR: My goal is simple. I am ready for my ten-year rejuvenation. I look and feel old. I missed my treatment at the 30- and 40-year mark because I was in jail and could not escape. As for accomplishments, none. I am a rebel. I protest and often go to prison. I inspire and recruit students. We put pressure on oligarchs and dictators to behave for a few years. We work hard, but ultimately, we fail. How can you overcome human greed? The powerful take too much and use that wealth to take more power. Humans are crap, as our surprising waiter alluded. Time to start over. The rich have no soul. For some of these greedy bastards, no amount of wealth will fill the empty place where their soul should be.

HYPATIA: You are honest, Fyodor. It is challenging to admit failures.

BILL: My millions became billions. I am one of the greedy. I have many simple tricks any fool could learn in 70 years of practice and study. While I have tricks to make money, I have no tricks to make me happy. I have great wealth. I have the power that Fyodor berates. I have a sense of accomplishment and feel like a winner, but I do not find my job fulfilling. I attain a quick win and feel happy for a few seconds, but the happiness does not last. The fine art, majestic homes, servants... none of it gives me the lasting pleasure of a glorious sunset or the smile on a beautiful young woman's face while I watch her hair blow in the wind. I spent ten lifetimes becoming richer, only to find more money in the bank is just a figure on a piece of paper. It does nothing. A nothing that grows into an increasingly vast bigger nothing.

FYODOR: What do you mean it does nothing?

BILL: I don't cure cancer. I don't feed the poor. I use the money to make more money, and it's a silly game. I am the king of a game that is no more than a scoreboard. In the market, every dollar I make is a dollar someone else lost. I did not create a new company. I may own shares for an hour or a few minutes. I hardly call that ownership. I make a million, and our greedy culture ensures people admire me. I make a billion; therefore, the culture demands people worship me more. They ask my opinion about everything. Somehow people think if I am rich, I am endowed with insight into what book, movie, or painting is good. I don't know about any of that stuff. I know about money. I am so one-dimensional. I probably hate myself more than Fyodor hates people like me. Fyodor calls me the soulless, and he may be right.

FYODOR: Hmm. We should talk. We really, really need to talk.

LEO: I love my life. I create beauty. I give people a song. A song does not hurt anyone. The music provides a few minutes of joy. I am not famous. I eschew fame. I sit in the backrooms and compose. I teach. I inspire musical children. I create little fugues that are mathematically perfect. I build symphonies from the shape of flowers like St. Anne's Lace. Each turn of the flower is a higher note, each dip a lower note. I take an inspiring painting of the sea or outer space, and I build a concert using each dot of the picture. A bright dot is a higher note, and a dark dot is a lower note. I seek out that mystical connection that makes notes or beats capture our feelings, our toes tap, our legs kick, and our hearts soar.

CELESTE: Wow. I never see your name in the newspapers or on TV. You would make more money if you were famous.

LEO: I have many stage names and companies that collect my royalties. I try to hide my age. Besides, I enjoy playing my songs in small groups. I improvise with musical friends. I love 12 people beating out a rhythm in unison on a bench in the park. The sense of being together. I experiment. I take joy by giving joy. I avoid fame to hide my age. We were told not to show the public we are immortal. We signed a contract.

HYPATIA: We will talk more about that contract. This reunion will be different than the last 300 years. I have always told you I cannot answer certain questions about the experiment you participated in. As we enjoy our tea, I will answer all your unanswered questions honestly and without reticence. For the first time, no secrets. Now, can someone pass me the ginger tea?

The group looks stunned. There is a long silence as people fuss with sugar and desserts for a few minutes.

FYODOR: I forgot how wonderful this indulgence is. Hmm, so good. I have lived amongst the poor and food insecure. People who wake up without knowing if they will eat that day. A slice of buttered toast feels like a small piece of heaven for half the world.

BILL: I have seven homes, but my favorite place is the park. I love to watch the children laugh about nothing. They run with such joy. The noise of laughter never bothers me. Have you tried these miniature meringues? They put strawberry juice between the meringue segments. Lovely.

HYPATIA: Celeste, are you playing footsie with Leo's groin while we eat?

CELESTE: What? Maybe? I dunno- so what if I am?

FYODOR: We never got an answer about our joints. Why is walking so difficult?

CELESTE: I can go to a dance. I look fantastic. I want to dance the tango under the moonlight. I am desperate to dance the salsa, twirl, and spin until I am sweaty and glued to my handsome partner. I look 18 and feel 18, and often a gorgeous yummy guy asks me to dance, but I cannot walk ten feet without two canes.

HYPATIA: It is AGE.

LEO: We all know it is aging, but why can't you fix it like you fixed how we look. No gray hair, wrinkles, or receding gums, but we cannot walk?

HYPATIA: Not aging, well, actually,.. hmm, yes, aging. I mean AGE is an acronym for *A*dvanced *G*lycation *E*nd products. Sugar in your system is cooked, making your ligaments stiff and brittle like crispy, overcooked meat. Your joints are cooked over the years with body heat. Heat and time.

CELESTE: That does not help. Explain it better.

HYPATIA: The joint immobilization histopathology is the expression of fibrotic genes because of increased pentosidine levels.

FYODOR: Huh?

LEO: What?

CELESTE: That explanation is not helping.

HYPATIA: I keep trying to explain a complex issue. Perhaps, this approach will work. You need sugar for energy, but sugar is cooking your joints. It is a tricky problem. I tried injecting ribose and changing the genes in collagen, but nothing improved the ROM.

BILL: ROM?

HYPATIA: Range of motion.

FYODOR: Hey, Hypatia, how can you tell the difference between male and female chromosomes?

HYPATIA: The X and Y chromosomes determine sex...

FYODOR: It is not that hard. You get the chromosomes to take down their genes, and you can see which is male or female.

HYPATIA: Groan and moan. That joke is so bad I want to unhear it.

FYODOR: I thought it was cute, Hypatia. Let's skip the science mumbo jumbo that tells us nothing. You said you would answer any question, even many questions you have refused to answer. Who paid for our treatments?

HYPATIA: Have you tried these scones with cream. I am always surprised by how they exceed my best memories. Oh, NASA paid for the study. A journey to the nearest planet where humans could survive would take over 100,000 years, even if we could move at 20% of the speed of light. They had to find a way to keep astronauts alive longer than a mere four score and ten years.

BILL: Can someone pass the champagne, please?

FYODOR: How many participants did you get in the study? Also, I always wanted to know if any people died from the treatments.

HYPATIA: That is a sad story. We had 29 studies that failed. Of course, we started with simple mammals like rats. The first successful rat trials were tested on small groups of five participants. About 50 people died during early human experiments.

BILL: Wow. You told us there were risks and side effects, but I had no idea test subjects were dying. How many people took our treatment and lived?

HYPATIA: Everyone who responded to our magazine advertisements and got version 30 lived. I tested first on five, then another round of 20, then another 100, and we kept going until we had 300 test subjects.

CELESTE: I thought you were teasing us when you said you would answer any question honestly. Hypatia, you are always full of surprises.

FYODOR: What is surprising is these cucumber and salmon sandwiches. Is that an apricot compote they added? This is a sensory journey. It has been decades since I ate something so delicious.

LEO: They are delicious but not as tasty as wine gums from England. To pontificate, I read with global warming that 90% of all species are dying. I hope wine gums do not go extinct. I also hope kale and squash go extinct soon, perhaps next week.

FYODOR: (*speaking with his mouth full*) How many of the 300 participants are still alive?

HYPATIA: Just the five of us. Almost immediately, people started dying, though not from treatment or old age. They died in car accidents, wars, or walking across a busy street. They died eating tainted food or slipping on an icy road. They died from being shot by a jilted lover or strangled by a cheated business partner. One was decapitated in a fall, and one got lost in the desert. One fellow was eaten by a bear in Alaska. Two died in an avalanche. Three were eaten by sharks, although in separate incidents. None of you are immortal. I cured the worst disease but did not provide the gift of immortality.

CELESTE: What disease? I have no disease.

HYPATIA: You all had the deadliest disease, 100% fatal, infecting 100% of us. I am talking about OAD, the Old Age Disease, the most lethal pandemic. I cured old age. The worst pandemic since mammals emerged from the mud was OAD. I should have been given a Nobel prize, but sadly, I had to sign the NDA, you know, the non-disclosure agreement. I can wail with teary eyes, but my Nobel prize is naught but a dream.

LEO: Hypatia, a magnificent achievement, but why all the secrecy?

FYODOR: Bill, stop hogging all the cream and pass me the dish. Old age does not kill everyone. Some people die of other stuff, such as waiting for a turn to take a little cream. I have been waiting forever.

BILL: It just feels like you are waiting forever. Forever is longer than two minutes.

FYODOR: Tell that to my mouth.

HYPATIA: True. Old age does not kill you if you die from something else. Old age only kills people who live long enough. As for secrets, I did not agree with the secrecy. Who amongst you are religious? Fyodor, you were dedicated to being the perfect Christian. You wanted to spread enlightenment and contentment to the unfortunate, just like Buddha, Yoda, Madonna, or Jesus. Celeste, your first marriage was in a church. Now, none of you talk about religion. What changed?

FYODOR: Fear of death. When you live hundreds of years, the need to believe in an afterlife becomes vague and remote. I am busy with more urgent stuff and not distant possibilities. I still think of myself as a good Christian, if somewhat lax of late. Though when I pray, I find I am talking to myself. Does that make god an imaginary friend, or am I becoming my own god?

BILL: You never give money to religions or go to holy sites. You never go to Church. You never talk about Church. I would call you a *functional atheist*.

FYODOR: That is a guilt nightmare. You are worse than a priest, Bill. I could say something mean, but I am too happy with the meal you bought me.

BILL: Show me your budget, Fyodor. With my expertise, I can tell what matters in your life in 30 seconds. Suppose someone claims to be a religious zealot but spends most of his money on booze and pornography. In that case, I'd say he is a boozy pornographer.

FYODOR: Gah. I am the good guy here. I am not a geographer.

BILL: Are you pretending you did not hear me, Fyodor? Americans claim they are religious, but they often dream about money, think about money, and even pray for money. I would say they worship the almighty dollar.

CELESTE: You are talking with your mouth full. I cannot hear you. Why is Fyodor becoming a geographer?

LEO: Not geographer. Bill said, a pornographer.

CELESTE: Oh, well, in jail, what else do they have except pornography.

FYODOR: (*standing*) I am not a pornographer. I am a justice warrior. Porno was just Bill's hypothetical example.

CELESTE: I never left my religion. I just stopped going. Science kept solving big problems, while thousands of years of prayer did not end the famines or the plagues. Synthetic fertilizer, hydroponics, robots... science was solving issues constantly, and prayer was not. You see it if you go to the hospital. Almost no one is waiting to talk to a priest. Five hundred rooms, 100 doctors, and one priest. People want a doctor to get a cure. Ninety-nine percent of the hospital is dedicated to scientific remedies. If prayer worked, we wouldn't need doctors. We would have 500 priests and one doctor.

LEO: I find spiritual moments in listening to music. I cannot describe the feeling. I feel elated and universally connected to the One lifeforce of all living things. It is effervescent. It is uplifting. I feel peace and joy at the same time.

HYPATIA: This was the reason for secrecy. We thought the outcry would rip society apart. Religion would decline if we had no fear of death. Why believe in an afterlife when you don't need it? What would happen to pension plans if all people lived twice as long? What would happen to overpopulation? The old might never retire, so the young people would never find jobs to build expertise and experience. How would we decide who wins the lottery of an endless lifespan?

FYODOR: The elites would take it all. Everyone knows that. The rest of us would die in the mud. The elites don't care; they would step over the bodies on the way to the bank. Exactly the way it is now in many poor nations.

LEO: Politicians would not get away with that for long. The people would demand it. They will not die with dignity in a dark corner. Dying with dignity is not in fashion today. The fight will be shrill enough to make past revolutions look like a debutante's ball.

CELESTE: Exactly. I would fight to the death to live.

FYODOR: Me too, although I would phrase that differently.

HYPATIA: Now you understand the secrecy.

LEO: Is Elvis still alive? Was he a test subject?

HYPATIA: Hitler and Elvis are dead, as far as I know.

CELESTE: Did anyone commit suicide?

HYPATIA: Yes, we lost about 30 of the 300 to suicide. The reason was not because they were tired of living or bored.

CELESTE: I know the reason.

LEO: What?

CELESTE: Love. They died of a broken heart, my dearest Leo. You love someone for 50 years, watch them get old, become feeble, and see their world shrink. They cannot run, then they cannot walk, and finally, they cannot sit up. With each change, their world becomes smaller. One day they run upstairs, and one day they are trapped on a bed. When you lose a love, you cannot breathe. You see them in every picture. You remember them wherever you go. You think you spot them in the crowd - but it is just someone who looks similar. It is hard to do once. It is unbearable to do it ten times. I need love to survive, but I am afraid to love another mortal. I have often thought of suicide.

LEO: Gosh, no. What stopped you?

CELESTE: The existential dilemma. Each day – I tell myself that I cannot do it today for some reason. I need to see the roses bloom one more time. It is always tomorrow. Tomorrow becomes today, but tomorrow is still a day away. Now comes, and now goes, but the now of right now is different than the now of 10 seconds ago. Now is constantly moving, and tomorrow is never within reach. Today is not a good day to die. The good news is I have a solution to my problem.

HYPATIA: What is the solution? This is a question I have grappled with often. I must know.

CELESTE: It is so easy and so obvious. I want... No, I need to love another immortal. I must love one of you. This is precisely why my stockinged foot is in Leo's firm, fine crotch, and it is such a fine crotch. He has the nicest crotch in the Southern Hemisphere.

Leo claps his hand over his eyes, then slaps his hand on the table.

LEO: Fine. You *only* love me because I am immortal. Move your foot.

FYODOR: Stop complaining. Open your mouth Leo, and taste a triple-layered angel cake. (*He flicks a handful of cake at Leo and hits him in the nose*). Celeste, I would worship your feet and every other bit of you, from your toes to those violet eyes and shiny hair. Let me be your crotchety crutch.

CELESTE: I would never see you. You'd be locked away or on the run from some murderous dictator. Dictators abound. They come scurrying out at night and steal the king's chair whenever people focus on sports or beer.

BILL: They always focus on sports and beer. If people stopped watching sports and paid attention, most politicians would be voted out. Rebellions would occur monthly.

FYODOR: You could persuade me to stay home, Celeste. You should choose me. Leo does not want your foot, but I do. I am the best bet.

BILL: Fyodor, it would only work for a few weeks, perhaps a century, but no longer. You are smitten with the blind Lady of Justice. You loved Lady Justice in childhood and love her still. Celeste, Fyodor gave you a false dichotomy.

LEO: Wait a minute. Hypatia, why not just freeze people, or make babies on a journey to a new planet. If you are frozen, you won't age as quickly. If we breed on the trip, our progeny discover the new world.

HYPATIA: Scientists are working on those ideas. However, there are some benefits to having a captain and at least one engineer awake, alive, and fixing issues as they happen.

CELESTE: What do you mean by a false dichotomy?

BILL: Would you like to wash my shoes or my car?

FYODOR: Take the shoes; shoes don't take as long to wash.

CELESTE: I take the car.

LEO: This is silly. Celeste, you are not restricted to just Fyodor or me. Never let someone limit you to two choices. You have a million options. You can be anyone. You can rule the world, run a company, or become an artist. People are always trying to limit a woman's choices.

BILL: Leo explains the false dichotomy well, Celeste. I might be interested in fixing your dilemma. I would not marry you for your money because I am already rich. I love you as you are. You have three immortal men, so three choices: Fyodor, Leo, or me.

HYPATIA: It is not a false dichotomy or a false trichotomy. You are all forgetting zero, nothing. She could choose Bill, Fyodor, Leo, or none of you. Celeste has four choices. People often forget nothing is an option, which is odd since nothing is what most people get most of the time. Some people get nothing almost all the time.

CELESTE: I have to think.

WAITER: The people at this table have the most bizarre conversations. I did not mean to eavesdrop, but you have many choices for a dessert wine. We have some fantastic ice wines from Canada. Of course, Celeste may have five choices as I count five men in this room.

HYPATIA: Six choices and counting. I am not married.

CELESTE: Really, Hypatia?

HYPATIA: Really.

FYODOR: What ice wine do you recommend?

WAITER: We have a sparkling ice wine, a red Cabernet Franc. Each sip is an explosion of taste. A bottle of sparkling ice wine is only available from one winery in Canada.

CELESTE: Bubbles are fun. If you add bubbles to anything, people laugh more. I will try the Cabernet while I consider my romantic options.

BILL: Bring glasses for everyone and a couple of bottles.

FYODOR: I can see Hypatia that you do not move with canes, braces, or crutches. If this glycation joint thing cannot be cured, how do you glide around so smoothly?

HYPATIA: Care to guess?

FYODOR: No. I desire to learn.

HYPATIA: I gave up on glucose browning. The solution is robotics and nanofibers. My knees and hips are fully robotic. The benefit is metal, gears, and pulleys keep me moving smoothly and without pain. The cost is I have no feeling at all below the knee. I have a sophisticated little chip in my brain that remotely connects to chips in my robotic joints. The solution is not ideal.

As long as I have a network connection and my battery keeps going, I can keep walking.

CELESTE: The waiter is out. He is not immortal.

HYPATIA: None of you are immortal. Your lives were merely extended. You will all die sooner than you think.

Leo/Celeste/Fyodor/BILL: What does that mean?

HYPATIA: No more treatments. The experiment has ended. We learned what we needed. You will age normally from this point and die like everyone else in a few decades.

CELESTE: (*wails*) No. No, no, no, no. I need to find my true love.

FYODOR: I have so much to do. I cannot die until social justice and inequality are solved. I have plans and plans within plans. I was about to study law, run for politics, and fix the system from within.

BILL: I cannot die. I haven't lived yet.

LEO: Seems reasonable. I had a good life.

(*Everyone looks at Leo*).

HYPATIA: Celeste, Fyodor, and Bill, you made no effort in the last 300 years to conceal your longevity. This was a breach of contract, so our contract with you is void. You have created too much social controversy and raised too many questions to continue. We do not have to meet again, and you will not be rejuvenated. Leo can get one treatment if he wants one since he was faithful to the secrecy clause.

CELESTE: Shrieking, I need love. I need a real, lasting love to feed my soul. I still want a child. How can I die childless?

BILL: Please, I will buy another treatment. I can pay $100,000 for one more treatment. No, a million. I will pay ten million for one more treatment. Think about what you could do with ten million. It could be our secret, Hypatia. I could give you cash, luxury yachts, or a prestige home.

HYPATIA: I love knowledge more than money. We have more significant issues than longevity. You have proved my method works. The old age disease is cured. We learned, and now science moves to the next challenge.

(*Wailing, shouting, screaming by all. Everyone is talking at the same time. Leo gets up and limps to the piano. The waiter comes out alarmed and runs from person to person. Celeste screams and faints on the floor. Leo begins to play Chopin's Revolutionary Etude which he morphs into a barrelhouse boogie*).

Curtain drops.

END OF ACT I

ACT II

FYODOR: Waiter, please bring me five bottles of champagne. I just learned I am dying. Hey folks, does anyone else want something while he is here? (*Some heads shake side-to-side, indicating 'no.' The waiter turns to leave*).

CELESTE: What did she mean we are not immortal? (*The waiter snaps forward again*).

WAITER: What do you mean by *what did she mean*?

FYODOR: Are you listening to our conversation?

BILL: Don't be mean, Fyodor. You know the waiter means no harm. You are just annoyed that Hypatia means to let us age.

Fyodor: Fine for you to say, Bill. You are a man of means. I am near 50 with no retirement savings.

CELESTE: You are talking in circles with different meanings of the word *mean*. Did she say we were not never immortal, or did she say we were not ever immortal? Don't be meanies. Now, I am doing it. Did she make a false statement? I have to know.

HYPATIA: *She* is sitting right here. The statement was not false.

FYODOR: If we are not never immortal, and that statement is not false, then we must be immortal. Not false is true. She added a negative, so not not false. If you calculate it, she is saying not not false, which reduces to not true, which is false. In other words, 'not never immortal' is true. Never immortal is mortal, so not ever immortal is not mortal, which is immortal. So, it is true we are all immortal. We have nothing to worry about.

BILL: OR, did she say 'not ever immortal' is not false. If her last statement is correctly saying the premise is not false, then it is true for being false as claimed. If it is true, then it is false since that is what the true statement stated. But if it is false, then it is true, as stated. Did I say that correctly? I am not sure. Seems messy? You may be right, Fyodor. We are still immortal.

HYPATIA: I am right here. You are overthinking it. You are not immortal; you are all dying. But don't worry about it. You will probably die of some other mishap long before you die of old age.

LEO: Reassuring as that is supposed to be, somehow the assurance I will be dead before I am old is not working for me.

HYPATIA: Men! This is not a logical conundrum to be solved. I cannot give you immortality, but I will give you a bigger penis if it makes you feel better. My most recent experiment had an exciting and unintended side effect. It makes a penis bigger.

FYODOR: You are telling me I will die, but I can be happy because I will die with a big schlong? How does that make it better? Will my penis still be big when I am dead? That is not the same as having a big penis while I'm alive. That is like saying you saved my damaged leg and put it in the fridge for safekeeping – in case I want it later. I don't want a leg in a refrigerator. I don't want a giant penis on my dead body.

HYPATIA: You don't seem at all pleased. I thought a giant penis was the most crucial thing in the world to men. Men are always doing strange things to prove you have the biggest dick. You buy a big truck to show your dick is bigger. You cut off another car to show your dick is bigger. You make endless dick jokes.

LEO: The tool size is less important than the performer's skill. The double bass is ten times the size of the violin, yet most men and women prefer the violin.

CELESTE: Oh, Leo. I do love you so much.

FYODOR: Kind offer as it is; I'd prefer another 50 years to another 5 inches. What would I do with a 15-inch penis, roll it into a ball and tape it to my leg so I don't scare the children?

HYPATIA: The Earth has 12 billion people, global warming has increased 2 degrees to crisis levels, and Fyodor will have 15 inches. Someone told me 93 percent of people believe numbers if you say them with confidence. I have found 93 percent of people agreed with this statement, so perhaps it is true?

BILL: Let's not be too hasty. I might take your offer. What I want most is both; a big penis and immortality?

FYODOR: Typical, the capitalist wants it all. Mine, mine, mine.

HYPATIA: Everyone spent 30 minutes in a panic. We are finally calming down enough to have a pleasant debate. We can enjoy a delicious meal and soothing tea.

CELESTE: Why now? In another 100 years, you would have more data? Scientists love data and AI almost more than people. Why not keep going for the data?

HYPATIA: That is the best argument. I made the exact same proposition when our project was canceled. Our first space travel challenge was living long enough, perhaps 100,000 years, to journey to the planet. The second challenge is radiation. Without an atmosphere in space, the human body is unprotected from solar radiation. A large solar flare would kill our astronaut pioneers. We can shield the spaceship but cannot prevent all radiation.

LEO: You didn't solve the 100,000-year challenge. We have lived a few hundred years, not a hundred thousand years.

HYPATIA: It comes down to distance. If we alter the human DNA, we can significantly expand the number of planets we can colonize and find a closer exoplanet. If we make you stronger, you could live on a planet with more gravity. On Earth, you might weigh 100 Kilograms. On Jupiter, you would weigh 2,000 Kilograms. As Fyodor suggested earlier, gravity would be so strong you could not lift your arm to scratch your ass. With bigger muscles, humans could live on Jupiter.

CELESTE: Exoplanet?

HYPATIA: An exoplanet is a planet that...

LEO: Sorry to interrupt, but that is too much. I could never walk or lift a finger if I was 2,000 pounds.

BILL: You don't walk now. Hobble, shuffle,... I would not call it a dapper walk or a saunter.

FYODOR: I felt like I weighed 2,000 pounds once. I was so constipated. Days and days. If you haven't had a good bowel movement for a week, you experience life differently. When I finally went, it was pure relief and joy. Nothing can beat a genuinely magnificent bowel movement when you have not gone for days. There are no words: Wordsworth, Byron, and even Shakespeare could not describe the tremendous relief and joy. I almost cried. Nothing beats an excellent bowel climax when you really need one.

CELESTE: Sounds like crap to me. We are eating. Change the subject, please.

HYPATIA: Exactly, Leo. We would need to alter human DNA to create a transhuman. If we change what it means to be human, we will have the strength to live on a giant planet.

FYODOR: Is there a third and fourth reason?

HYPATIA: Yes. If you had stronger lungs, you could live in a denser atmosphere. If you had gills, you could live on a water planet. If we make humans kinder and more compassionate, we could survive longer on a confined spaceship. As Fyodor said, some humans are greedy and self-centered.

CELESTE: This whole space travel thing is too hard. Tell me again, what are exoplanets?

HYPATIA: Exoplanets are planets that orbit around other stars. We are focused on finding exoplanets that humans can live on. Space challenges are too difficult for humans but not for superhumans. We can take DNA from animals to make a better human. No species could survive space travel without some DNA alterations. It is technically impossible to send a mere human into deep space without DNA improvements.

LEO: We prevent humans from going extinct by creating superhumans. Is this not the same as making humans extinct? Won't the superhumans make us extinct?

FYODOR: Exactly, Leo. Where are the older versions of man, for example, Cro-Magnons, Neanderthals, or Australopithecus? They are extinct. Homosapiens are killers.

HYPATIA: I know. Such a shame. We could have tested drugs on those earlier versions of humans. A test on a Cro-Magnon would be much better than a chimpanzee.

CELESTE: That is horrible. We prevent extinction so we can do better lab tests.

HYPATIA: Just saying. I did lab tests on all of you. You were my participants. I wish I could have experimented on Neanderthals first. Neanderthals are stronger than homosapiens.

BILL: I have heard this kind of speech before. Only outstanding test pilots with the 'right stuff' can be astronauts. If I recall, monkeys were sent into space; dogs were the first astronauts, and they did just fine. We don't need super-trained test pilots if a monkey can do it. Any slob civilian will do.

CELESTE: But where does that leave us?

HYPATIA: Humans have been evolving for millions of years. We continually evolve. We evolved from protozoa to mammals, mammals to humans, and now humans to transhumans. We are speeding up the process. You will be the quaint old humans once we improve the human genome. We can evolve by accident or design, but we must evolve or go extinct.

BILL: You didn't answer my question. Any monkey can travel in space. Scientists like to keep tweaking nature and playing God.

HYPATIA: Bill, we cannot save the human race by sending a monkey across the universe. The Earth is a dangerous place. God, or Nature if you prefer, can throw out an earthquake, a tsunami, a few hurricanes, some famines, and a few pandemics at any time. The global climate crisis has created a cascade of positive feedback loops. We must get into space, or humans will become extinct for sure. Monkeys in space won't fix that issue. All our knowledge, our technology, could be lost in seconds.

BILL: Goddess Hypatia has decreed. Leo can live. The rest of us must die.

HYPATIA: Did we play God when we planted fields instead of collecting berries where we found them? Did we play God when we transplanted a new kidney into the Pope? He had a lot to say about transplants before he needed one. Now the silence is deafening. Was I playing God when I repeatedly reset the telomere on your cells and gave you 300 years of life? Now you are concerned about God -now that you are dying as nature designed. You were non-religious, but now you are dying; it took only 10 minutes to become religious again.

FYODOR: What are these little cakes with the flakey pastry, custard, and cream filling? They are delicious.

LEO: They are called Neapolitans.

FYODOR: I am going to order another five. Does anyone else want one?

BILL: I suppose I will have one.

FYODOR: Okay, six Neapolitans, two bottles of cherry brandy, and I want a bowl of these chocolate cherries. (*Fyodor grabbed his crutches and zoomed over to the waiter's screen*).

CELESTE: I think you should send me into space. I am already lovely. People love me.

BILL: Don't forget we are your most successful test subjects. Of the 300, only we survived. More importantly, we are all successful. What we do, we do extraordinarily well. Leo is fantastic. Hypatia, you are the most incredible scientist ever, given you cured old age. Hypatia, you should send us. We are proven winners.

HYPATIA: I am not the most incredible scientist. I stand on the shoulders of 500 years of scientists. You are using a fallacy-fallacy.

LEO: I usually get this stuff, but what is a fallacy-fallacy? Did you stutter?

HYPATIA: When you think an idea is wrong because the logic is wrong, that is a fallacy fallacy. It is a fallacy to say a conclusion is incorrect because the logic is fallacious. Someone can create nonsense in every argument and make logical errors throughout but still propose a correct conclusion. The conclusion may be a correct statement by pure luck.

CELESTE: I am very skilled at fallacious. Men love it when I give them a fallacious.

BILL: I read about fallacy fallacy. Isn't that one from Aristotle. No, I'm confused. It was Aristotle's drunk uncle, Dolus, who talked about fallacy-fallacy.

HYPATIA: (*ignores Bill and gives Celeste a look*). Take an example. Whenever the shipments of bananas go up, the number of babies goes up. The conclusion is shipments of bananas cause babies.

CELESTE: Well, that is wrong. Kissing causes babies. Not immediately, there are a few more steps in between, but it starts with a kiss, and in nine months, you get a baby. I often wanted a baby after kissing. Sadly, my hope was disappointed.

LEO: Yeah, I get it. It is a fallacy to say bananas cause babies. The error is called a false cause, I think.

HYPATIA: True, Leo. The logic is wrong. Celeste is right. Sex causes babies, but the conclusion is insightful. Babies have no teeth. Babies like soft foods like bananas. The more babies we have, the more bananas we buy, so shipments of bananas increase with more babies. Bananas don't cause babies, but the numbers of babies and bananas increase together. The data is correlated, but the conclusion is wrong. Still, it does have a glimmer of insight buried in the conclusion.

BILL: Hypatia, you cured old age. Alchemists, scientists, and a million charlatans tried and failed to do what you have done. You succeeded where thousands of years and thousands of scientists have failed. You are brilliant.

HYPATIA: Were you going to add, 'for a woman or a black person'?

BILL: Why are you putting words into my mouth?

LEO: Hypatia, you are the best of us, the best of all of us. Man or woman, black or white, young or old, you are the most brilliant. Period.

HYPATIA: Interesting. I expected the outcry. I expected bargaining and personal attacks. I did not expect this approach.

(*Fyodor returns, somehow walking on crutches while eating a pastry simultaneously. The waiter follows with a tray of cherries and brandies*).

FYODOR: This is better than I remembered.

CELESTE: You were eating that pastry two minutes ago.

FYODOR: I know, and it is even better now.

HYPATIA: I was expecting an *ad hominem* attack. You know. I must rejuvenate you, or I am a nasty bitch, with many insults, a few threats, and that kind of stuff. Instead, you give me a reverse ad hominem. I should send you, not because I am nasty if I don't, but because Celeste is kind and wonderful, Bill is successful, and I am brilliant.

FYODOR: I want to toast Bill; without you, I would be dining on beans from a can. I want to toast all of you. You are kind and wonderful. This is perhaps the best night of my miserable life.

CELESTE: No one has taken a 100,000-year journey into space. We have no knowledge or experience about such a journey. We don't know what will work. Hypatia, you have no data, fundamental theories, or empirical evidence. You should send us. We are your best hope. The history of supermen and uber-humans is not good.

HYPATIA: Wow. I am impressed. First, the reverse ad hominem attack, and now you move the burden of proof to me. You are asking me to prove you could not make the trip. Clever.

FYODOR: Why is that clever?

HYPATIA: It is a fallacy of ignorance. We don't know what will work. Therefore, I am being asked to disprove *your* idea instead of proving *my* idea. You are asking me to show non-existing evidence for my not being right. How can I disprove a hypothesis that has no data?

FYODOR: If I am honest, and I am, I say shut up and let the serious eating and drinking begin. We can get into politics and debates at 2 AM when we are good and drunk. You know what would look good on you, Celeste.

CELESTE: What?

FYODOR: Me.

CELESTE: That is a horrible joke.

FYODOR: (*Grabs his stomach, holds his hand up for silence, then burps loudly for a long time*). Not so horrible, and not a joke.

HYPATIA: I could spend a thousand lifetimes proving what does not work. It is not helpful. Better to spend a few years proving what does work than test the 200 million billion ideas that don't work. We call this Ockham's Razor. He says always propose and test the simplest solution. We grasp his concept but don't know how to spell his name. History shows many inventive spellings. Perhaps an example to illustrate. When my dog takes a big poop, flies take less than two seconds to show up. How can they find the poop so fast? I look around before the poop. I never see a fly for 50 yards in any direction. Dog poops. Suddenly, three files appear in two seconds. The only possibility, flies must come from another dimension, a parallel universe, to get there so quickly. Dog poops. Inter-dimensional poop detector activates, and three flies teleport to the poop. Obviously, they had to be waiting in another dimension. If not, I would see them coming.

FYODOR: That's what I wanted - drinking and talking poop. Flies from another dimension is silly.

LEO: Laughing, where is your proof?

HYPATIA: Prove I am wrong. I dare you. Show me your theory proving dimensional portals for flies is not valid. See. I moved the burden of proof to you. Now you are working from ignorance and must prove my crazy ideas are wrong. It's a trick. I don't have to prove you are the best team for the space journey. You came up with that idea, so you must show reasons and proof to support your own views. It is not my job to prove you are wrong. It is your job to prove you are right.

FYODOR: Talk, talk, talk. How can you talk about all these ideas when the most fantastic foods and drinks are in front of us. Stop talking. Rejoice in our bounty. Live now. This is my happiest moment. Being with you and you and you. I love you all. I love you, Celeste. I love you, Leo (*Fyodor struggles to stand on his chair*). Ladies and gentlemen, friends and lovers, to the honorable and the dishonorable, I propose a toast to us. (*He wipes away a tear*). To the immortals, to us! (*Fyodor takes a swig from his brandy and tosses a chocolate cherry high. He tips his head back, and the cherry goes down the wrong way. Fyodor starts to choke. He waves his hand, turns a bit blue, starts coughing hard, then topples down. Bill and Leo jump to his aid, but Fyodor is too heavy. Fyodor is on his knees).*

CELESTE: Is he kidding, or is this real?

BILL: He made this joke to us once before, but this looks different.

(Hypatia swoops in, reaches into his throat, and tries to scoop out the cherry but fails because her fingers are not long enough, and he is too heavy to move).

CELESTE: Is he okay?

HYPATIA: He is dead. As I was saying, we are not immortal.

(Everyone sits quietly for a minute and stares vacantly).

LEO: He died happily. He said it was his happiest moment.

CELESTE: He said he loved me. He is the first immortal to love me.

HYPATIA: This immortal is dead. I believe this is proof he was mortal.

BILL: Death by chocolate cherry; not what I expected for a justice warrior. I thought it would be a noble battle, not an insidious cherry.

WAITER: What's happened?

HYPATIA: Sadly, our friend is dead. I think it was gluttony and misfortune, and now there are four.

WAITER: I will call Security.

CELESTE: He was so full of life; just like that, he is gone. Life is hard.

LEO: Would anyone like a chocolate cherry?

Bill, Celeste, HYPATIA: NO!

LEO: I think it is safe. It is improbable cherries will kill more of us in the same evening.

HYPATIA: Twenty-five thousand Americans die from choking on food each year. A common way to pass is throwing food in the air, which goes down the wrong way. Ninety-three percent of people believe that.

LEO: I read most people die in their sleep. I never realized until I read that headline that sleeping is the most dangerous thing we do. Sleeping and eating. How did we make it this long?

CELESTE: I cannot wait any longer. I have to pee in the worst way. (*She struggled to pull her two canes from under the table. It took a few minutes for her to position the canes, get up, get her balance, and hobble to the bathroom behind the screen*).

CELESTE: I love to be looked at, but not now. Look away. I can't navigate around Fyodor. This is too difficult.

(*They exchanged glances. Celeste looks 18, a stunning beauty but in obvious pain*).

HYPATIA: You do know that study does not say sleeping is dangerous. You made two mistakes, a hasty generalization and a false cause. The facts are correct, but your conclusion is wrong. We spend an average of eight hours sleeping every 24 hours. If you spend 16 hours a day reading, the chance of dying when reading would be greater than sleeping. It is *not* the reading that kills you. Death by reading is not a thing. Death by cancer or heart attack might kill you. When you die, it will most likely happen when you are doing something you do often, such as sleeping.

LEO: I knew that - sort of. It is so obvious when you say it that way. This seems like a good time to exit. I will go to the men's bathroom but not for a bath. My leg goes stiff if I sit too long.

WAITER: Where did the other two go? Security says no one must leave until they have examined the body.

BILL: They just went to the bathroom. They went right by your station.

WAITER: Good. Can I get you anything while you wait?

BILL: We are good for now. Fyodor ordered all this food and drink before he left the realm of the living.

HYPATIA: What do you think?

BILL: About what?

HYPATIA: About all of it. Everything. Life, love, superhumans, space travel, death, and chocolate cherries, if you like.

BILL: I am still thinking about Fyodor. Gone just like that.

HYPATIA: I am not a fan of chocolate cherries. I like to see my fruit before I eat it. I want to see if the cherry is fuzzy green instead of bright red. If it is covered in chocolate. It could be an ex-cherry, more of a chocolate-covered fungus fuzz-ball than cherry.

BILL: True. Honestly, at this particular moment, I am a bit off of the whole cherry thing. I don't believe in heaven. I would prefer to go to a beach than heaven if given a choice. As you know, Miami has been 10 feet below sea level since the global warming crisis hit hard. I bought a cottage on a Canadian beach. Beautiful sunsets and sunshine. Not the blistering deserts of Ohio and Indiana. You should join me in Canada if you have a few holidays.

HYPATIA: Sure, at the summer's end when the wildfires are subsiding. I thought it was impossible to get into Canada, given they still have fresh water and most countries don't.

BILL: I own property in Canada. I can get you in.

WAITER: Sorry to interrupt. My real name is Detective Pierre Sartre, and I am with the Immigration Department. I replaced the actual waiter tonight, and we canceled other guests. We suspected your dead friend of being an Iranian spy. We saw him on one of our surveillance drones. He was on an Iranian fishing trawler just outside our territorial waters. He swam fifteen miles to our shore without going through immigration or customs.

BILL: Fifteen miles. That is a long way in the chilly waters of December.

SARTRE: He had an intelligent plan. He covered his whole body with a thick layer of lard. The lard worked like blubber on a whale and, locked in his body heat, made him buoyant, and kept much of his skin from getting wet. He hid behind a small 20-centimeter buoy to stay afloat and avoid detection. He kicked his way to shore as if the buoy was simply abandoned and floating randomly. We initially saw nothing until the infrared setting on the drone detected the heat of a being instead of nothing but a buoy.

(*A woman's voice moaned softly, getting more intense, then muffled. The silkscreen started to rock a little at first, then aggressively. The moans grew louder.* Everyone at the table exchanged glances. Leo and Celeste emerged. *Leo's shirt was half-tucked into his pants, Celeste had a pearl necklace hanging over one shoulder, and her hair was lopsided. Leo had lipstick on his chin. The two of them limped and shuffled to their chairs. Celeste was flushed*).

CELESTE: Did I miss anything?

HYPATIA: I was wondering the same thing. Am I missing out?

BILL: I know I missed something, and so did Detective Sartre. He is from the Immigration Department.

CELESTE: Do you mean the waiter?

BILL: You see, Sartre, Fyodor escaped from Iran's Evin prison. I am sure his passport, identification, and money were seized on his arrest. He could not just walk up to our border agent without identification, especially if Iran monitors travel bookings and border crossings. He could stow away on a fishing vessel without his documents and bribe them to drop him offshore. He is a citizen of our country. Everyone here can vouch for him. Since he is dead, we have no reason to lie. Our nation is safe.

SARTRE: I will need a sworn affidavit from any two of you. Each of you must give me identification details before you leave. We will do an autopsy for the cause of death. Do you need more drinks, or should I bring the cheque?

BILL: One cheque for the table. You can join us if you like, detective. Also, please move the body as soon as you can. It is hard to have fun with a dead friend watching. Besides, I just found out we are all dying.

SARTRE: Of course, Sir. Sorry to hear you are all dying.

BILL: You are an excellent waiter, Sartre. I will tip accordingly. Is this your first time as a waiter?

SARTRE: Yes, Sir. I usually chase down felons, outsmart smugglers, or read in the library. My clients don't give me tips in currency, although I get a lot of verbal tips from criminals trying to use me to shut down their competition.

BILL: You think of criminals as clients?

SARTRE: Without criminals, we would not need police, judges, or jailors. We'd have no need for criminal lawyers, prosecutors, or bailiffs.

CELESTE: What do you read in the library? Do you like any romantic comedies?

SARTRE: Some people think it is a nauseous way to learn, but I am self-taught at the library. I got the idea from a book written by a French philosopher. I started by reading all the authors in the A section. I am now reading the N authors. I am well-educated in the thinkers below O. I know Aristotle and Jane Austen. I have read Bacon and Berkeley, Hegel, Kant, and Nietzsche. I have read nothing from Zeno, of course. My knowledge of Zoroastrian is zero.

LEO: Me too. I am not up on my Zoroastrian. Something to do with the force of light versus dark. It makes me think of the movie Star Wars. '*The dark side has power, Luke.*' I used Zoroastrians in hypothetical questions because I did not want to offend any group. One evening, I met an actual Zoroastrian. Apparently, Zoroastrians are in Iran, which was once part of the Persian empire. Given Fyodor's time in Iran, I bet our dead Fyodor could tell us about Zoroastrians, a religion that predated Christianity.

SARTRE: Yes. We were sure Fyodor would lead us to some spy network instead of a dead end.

HYPATIA: A dead end for Fyodor, aptly put.

CELESTE: Hypatia, I wanted to ask you about the transhuman space journey. What standard are you using to select future superhumans?

(*Bill, Leo, and Celeste lean in to hear better*).

HYPATIA: I am so glad you asked. A remarkable story about how science works. As I told you, we started with the muscles. Roughly speaking, for every 100,000 births, you get a mutation, and for every 100,000 genetic mutations, you get a favorable mutation. Most mutations make an animal weaker, perhaps deformed. On rare occasions, the species is improved. We had some mutated mice in the lab that were born strong. Really, really strong.

Bill, Leo, and CELESTE: (*together*) Really, mighty mice.

HYPATIA: Big bulging mice muscles. Schwarzenegger mice. Pure accident of nature. We quickly did a genetic study, identifying any genes different from normal mice. Success. We identified a single gene mutation. Next, we checked if humans had the same gene and made the exact DNA change in people suffering from degenerative muscle diseases. Again, success. People whose muscles were wasting away were cured. Not part of the plan, but athletes with perfectly normal genes wanted the mighty mouse mutation. Gene therapy changing a single gene won't show up on drug tests. We are creating humans with double the strength. It does not help joints, but it is precisely what we do to develop trans-humans.

(*Bill, Leo, and Celeste lean back. Disappointed*).

LEO: Super mice. Great. Why not make a boot-proof cockroach instead of giving us working joints? What would happen if a gene mutated and the cockroach became squash-proof. Jump on him with both boots, he shrugs and keeps scurrying along to the nearest drain.

HYPATIA: That would be stupid. We are already overrun by roaches. That would make it worse.

CELESTE: Instead, we have super strong mice that can punch a hole in my wall and carry away five bags of beans on their backs with each trip.

BILL: Exactly. Scary.

CELESTE: The only way to fix my joints is to cut my nerves and get a robot leg? I won't buy dancing shoes today. Now, how about the standard to qualify for the NASA team?

HYPATIA: We have a standard, and none of you qualify. You cannot walk without assistance. We need someone who can survive radiation, live long, and handle high gravity or a thick atmosphere. Walking is a definite requirement to explore planets. Although given you would be weightless in space, you may have a point for the journey but not the colonization. You could never disembark. A one-way ticket to Neverland.

LEO: Now, the catch. Is there a standard for making that standard for selection, or will any old standard do?

HYPATIA: That is a good question. I don't think they have a standard in the standards team for making new standards. I know they collated data and set some targets.

LEO: Are you telling me that fancy pants NASA have no standard for making standards?

HYPATIA: No. Nooo, not really. You have identified a weakness in our selection criteria.

LEO: If you have no standards for making standards, I bet you have no standards for the people making the standards for the standards team.

HYPATIA: I see where this is going. The recess problem. You are going ask if there are standards for the standards of standards making standards going all the way down to the first standard published about keeping the cave opening clear of garbage such as mammoth bones and saber tooth tiger droppings?

LEO: Exactly, so we should be allowed to be part of the team. You clearly don't have enough standards. You need a benchmark.

HYPATIA: The universe came from a Big Bang. Where did the Big Bang come from? Someone pushed the first domino to start the long chain of collapsing dominos. Something or someone created the Big Bang. The someone was the Unmoved Mover, according to Aristotle. This mover was not moved by a prior force. Was it God? If I say yes, you will ask me who created God, and who created the God that created God, to the bigger God, before Zeus, before the Titans, before the most significant, most grand, most infinite, and most mighty of the mighty Gods of all the Gods before our current Gods.

LEO: Exactly. And when you get to the God of Gods, you still have the same question. Who created the first Goddess, our Mother Earth of the Big Bang Birth. Who gave birth to that most mighty of almighty Gods, Father Sky, the most extraordinary God of the Corn Bird, as the Aztecs might claim. Who created the first standard used to make all other standards.

HYPATIA: A circle, to be sure. Did it all start with the chicken or the egg, my friends?

LEO: Finally, submission. Now, will you rejuvenate all of us?

HYPATIA: I could make the same argument for many things. How can I understand your words? You use words to explain other words. Words are used to understand words; if we track backward, we return to the first word used to define the second word. Full circle.

LEO: You understand perfectly. The Circle of the Life of Words.

HYPATIA: Let's have the Un-circle of Life. We will spin back to the first word, but the proof is in the empirical evidence. I understand your words, even if the words within words using words are drawn in a circle or undrawn in a circle. Circle or not. I understand you. You understand me. The cycle of endless cycles within cycles does not matter. We have a functional language. I talk. You talk. We hear. Proof of the pudding is in the wording. We decided, somewhere, to limit how many recessive cycles to take.

CELESTE: Some people talk, and no one listens. Some people speak without words – they use gestures and symbols. I think some people fall in love with just a look. No words. No sounds. They gaze into your eyes, and we communicate desire perfectly.

LEO: Hmm. So Hypatia, you get us from one word to a whole language but skip steps 2 to 2,000 because those words are missing.

HYPATIA: An exciting game.

HYPATIA: Do you remember the famous equation E = E?

BILL: It is true E = E. That is a tautology. 1 = 1. I can do this all day. Bill = Bill. The equation only became interesting when Einstein went from $E = E$ to $E = mc^2$.

HYPATIA: Exactly. We don't need to understand every machine, every beginning, and every end, to push the silly button. Push the button, and start vacuuming the carpet, even if you don't know how vacuums work. No recess tricks allowed. You can vacuum without understanding who created the vacuum or the first god or the last god.

SARTRE: Hi, folks. Something a bit odd about these identification papers. Leo, you gave us the Artists Union membership card showing you have been a member for 22 years. Hypatia, you gave us an Employee card for NASA with no birth date. Both these documents check out. Bill, you gave us a driver's license showing your birth date, which says you are 30. When I look carefully at your birth year, it seems you altered a 3 into an 8, which would make you hundreds of years older? Celeste, you gave us a marriage certificate clearly stating your birth more than 300 years ago. I think we are looking at fake documents. No one is over 300; I can see you are not 300. You look barely old enough to drink or drive, Celeste.

CELESTE: I thought 300 was old enough to drive?

SARTRE: This is serious.

CELESTE: I understand. Am I free to drive away if I prove I am over 300?

SARTRE: I won't tell you again. This is serious.

HYPATIA: I don't mean to interrupt, but the weightless option is good. You could live 100,000 years, or perhaps 50,000, if we find a closer planet. Your joints would be almost free of pain in a weightless space. Fifty thousand years of life is a good option compared to 50.

CELESTE: I will go if Leo comes with me. He would be my brave and dashing ship captain. He could tie me to the steering wheel and strip me naked. When we are not playing pirates, I could do the engineering job. Learning aeronautical engineering might take four or five years, but I don't see that as challenging. I am a quick learner when motivated by another 50,000 years of love. Leo could learn to fly better than the space monkeys. He is a wizard on the keyboards, and flying has a lot of buttons and dials.

BILL: NASA will want more assurance than 'I am a quick learner.' What is your proof, Celeste?

CELESTE: To please my fourth husband, I became fluent in Greek in 21 days.

BILL: Celeste, learning engineering takes a different skill set than learning languages.

CELESTE: You don't know me as much as you should, Bill. My sixth husband was an engineer, and we always discussed his work problems over dinner. Anyone can pick up a book, read it, and learn from it. I helped him with some of his publications. I was simply shy about my contributions.

HYPATIA: We have a few challenges to work out. With a weightless environment, you will lose bone density. You will get shorter and shorter and eventually become a big blob resembling a jellyfish within 50,000 years.

CELESTE: Ugh. We need to fix that.

HYPATIA: Your bones won't hurt, but they may be spongy instead of rigid.

CELESTE: We most definitely need to fix that. I don't want to lose my curvy shape. I will take that as an engineering challenge. We can use centrifugal force to create artificial gravity.

BILL: That is a good idea, but your joints will hurt.

HYPATIA: I am sure Celeste will be the sexiest blob in space. Of that, I have no doubt.

SARTRE: It is a big mistake to keep ignoring me.

HYPATIA: Done, folks. If you get the needed education, I will find a way to get you the job. Somehow, I will make it happen. Leo and Celeste will be plan A, and we will have plans B, C, D, and E if the unexpected happens.

SARTRE: That's it. I am going to file a Subpoena to Appear.

HYPATIA: Before you do a lot of paperwork, Sartre. I need you to first sign some confidentiality documents required by the government. You have to be read into the program. Once you sign, I can provide you with documentation and proof of life for Bill and Celeste. One trip to NASA, and we can settle the whole matter. One minor consideration, a non-disclosure document is required. You will not be able to talk about it.

SARTRE: I will collect the documentation, but how can I prosecute if I cannot talk about it.

HYPATIA: That is a complication, but if their documentation is correct, there is no identity crime and no need to prosecute.

CELESTE: What about the radiation problem?

SARTRE: Radiation problem? Did Fyodor smuggle Iranian nuclear radioactive materials?

HYPATIA: I will find a solution. We could have a safe capsule to wait out large solar flares or storms. For regular radiation, we could redirect most of it to a solar sail that accelerates the spacecraft. I am not in charge of the program, but I am influential. We will launch into space to find an exoplanet. We will also launch the longest, most adventuresome, most dedicated love story in the history of humankind, a marriage with 50,000 to 100,000 anniversaries. After that moment behind the bouncing waiter's screen, how could we deny your passion?

LEO: Did you propose marriage on my behalf, commit me to return to university for another degree, sign me up as an astronaut, and commit me to a 50,000-year employment contract?

CELESTE and HYPATIA: Yes. I believe that is the main idea.

LEO: Okay. Sounds perfect.

SARTRE: WHAT RADIATION? I am nothing. I am a human being. I exist. I won't be ignored. I have an essence. Who has the radioactive materials?

HYPATIA: The sun provides solar radiation. Our atmosphere keeps us safe. When the ozone layer in our atmosphere got a hole during the 1990s because of toxic pollutants, the rate of skin cancer in Australia jumped by 300%. In space, there is no atmosphere to block solar radiation. Solar radiation can be deadly.

SARTRE: Oh, that radiation.

CELESTE: Thank you, Hypatia. Leo and I could have 100,000 years of incredible, sumptuous love, plus or minus a few thousand - and the added bonus of a near-weightless environment, so our joints won't hurt so much. Think Leo; the stars will be closer and brighter. I will literally and figuratively float in your arms for endless nights.

HYPATIA: By my rough calculation, 18 million and 250 thousand nights, perhaps twice that if the journey takes 100,000 years.

BILL: Much as I love you, Celeste, this is too big a commitment, even for me.

LEO: I am more of a night person. Celeste, I accept your proposal with a smile, a flutter in my heart, and your foot still in my groin. We will be happy. *(He moves and sits next to Celeste and snuggles against her kissing her nose for a laugh and then her neck with a moment becoming a minute of passion. He kisses her neck repeatedly).*

SARTRE: You are an odd group. I feel as if I am in some strange stage play setup solely to embarrass me. Is this an elaborate practical joke? Just confirm, Chief Camus at the office did not author this exceedingly bizarre story? He likes these intricate attempts at existential humor. Am I the victim? Immortal love in space? Is any of this true?

HYPATIA: You may never know unless you sign the non-disclosure agreement, Sartre.

FADE OUT.

THE END

www.ingramcontent.com/pod-product-compliance
Lightning Source LLC
Chambersburg PA
CBHW030828060726
47590CB00004B/1444